the
ARCTIC

All photographs were taken by Francis Latreille,
except for those on pages 16–17: © Akg-images

Production Manager: Colin Hough-Trapp

Library of Congress Cataloging-in-Publication Data:
Latreille, Francis.
[Paradis blanc. English]
The Arctic / by Francis Latreille.
p. cm.
ISBN-13: 978-0-8109-1428-5
ISBN-10: 0-8109-1428-X
1. Arctic regions—Description and travel—Juvenile literature. I. Title.
G614.L35 2006
910.911'3—dc22
2006015303

Printed and bound in Belgium
10 9 8 7 6 5 4 3 2 1

HNA ▌▌▌▌▌
harry n. abrams, inc.
a subsidiary of La Martinière Groupe
115 West 18th Street
New York, NY 10011
www.hnabooks.com

the ARCTIC

Photographs by Francis Latreille

Text by Catherine Guigon

Illustrations by Frédéric Malenfer

Abrams Books for Young Readers

New York

CONTENTS

How Were These Pictures Taken? 4

The Lands of the Far North 6

The Regions of the Far North 8

Sea Ice in Perpetual Motion 10

Breaking the Ice Sheet 12

The People of the Far North 14

A Long Migration Toward the East 16

Seals Populate the Ice Shelf 18

The Discovery of the Arctic 20

The Conquest of the North Pole 22

Bitter Cold 24

The Work of the Wind 26

Dressing Warmly 28

His Majesty the Polar Bear 30

Hunting with the Inuits 32

The *Inlandis* of Greenland 34

Cathedrals of Ice 36

In the Wake of the Whale 38

Color in the Night 40

The Dolgans: Nomads of the Tundra 42

The Reindeer of the Tundra 44

A Day in the Life of the Dolgans 46

The Polar Night 48

Siberian Festival 50

The Arctic Summer 52

A Herd of Musk Oxen 54

Pacifying the Evil Spirits 56

A Mammoth Called Jarkov 58

Scientific Expeditions 60

Heat Wave in the Arctic 62

The Threat to Animal Life 64

The Polar World Adrift 66

The Future of the Great North 68

How Were These Pictures Taken?

It's not easy to explore the frozen regions of the Far North. Your fingers go numb in the cold. Blizzards try to tear the camera from your hands. But Francis has fallen in love with the changing light of the Arctic and thinks a Polar expedition is a real treat!

Francis first saw the beauty of a frozen landscape when he was six; the winter in the Loire Valley was savage and the thermometer went down to –4° Fahrenheit. One morning, he saw white "pancakes" spreading over the river's surface: ice was forming. When the ice solidified, he wrapped up in warm clothes and went out to skate on the river. That was his first experience of venturing out on the ice, and the memory has never left him.

Years later, when he became a famous photographer, Francis had the chance to accompany the famous explorer and doctor Jean-Louis Étienne on a mission to the North Pole. It was an ordeal. His feet slipped on the powdery snow, and his fingers froze. But his childhood love of icy landscapes survived. Now he adores the magical light of the tundra, the frozen waste of the north, and the Northern Lights.

The Arctic is one of the last wild places left on the planet. There are no roads or railways there. Wherever he went, Francis used the local means of transport: snowmobiles or sleighs drawn by dogs or reindeer. Long distances are covered by helicopter or boat—and sometimes the boat is an icebreaker.

To survive on your own in the polar region is quite an adventure. You need a lot of equipment. Francis slept under canvas in a top-quality sleeping bag made from the down (inner feathers) of geese or eider ducks. (That is where we get the word *eiderdown*!) He dressed in lots of thin, warm layers: cotton on the inside, wool and fleece next, then windproofs. But the most important thing is to not run out of kerosene. All the water in the Arctic is frozen and has to be melted for drinking. Moreover, you need hot food, and most of your food is dehydrated, freeze-dried, or in powder, so you need water to prepare it. You have to carry about two pounds of food per person per day. Cameras are sensitive to the cold; below −13° Fahrenheit, film becomes very brittle and batteries quickly run down. And you must be careful to avoid sudden changes of temperature: when you come into a heated room, condensation may form in the camera lens and damage it.

The Far North also has one or two surprises in store—like the day Francis found himself face to face with a polar bear! He had to beat a hasty retreat, dumping his equipment. Fortunately, his pilot spotted the danger and set the helicopter blades revolving to frighten the bear off. Francis was saved, but it was very frightening! Unlike the polar bears, the people who live in the Far North are very friendly. Francis does not speak Inuit, Sámi, or Dolgan, but he always managed to make friends. If you want to communicate, be patient, thoughtful, and smile a lot—or learn the language!

The Lands of the Far North

The Climate of the Far North

The climate of the Far North is polar; that is, very, very cold. In winter the average temperature is −13° Fahrenheit, and in summer 50° is about the maximum. The air is dry because the Arctic Ocean is under a bank of ice most of the time and does not evaporate. Different kinds of ice form: The ice shelf, or sea ice, is saline because it is made of sea water, which freezes at 28° Fahrenheit. Glacier ice, made of packed snow, is fresh water. These glaciers constitute the ice cap, or *inlandis*, which covers most of Greenland apart from its coasts. Where these glaciers meet the coast, they produce icebergs: great blocks of frozen fresh water that have broken off to float away in the sea.

The Peoples of the Far North

In the past, the natives of the Far North were nomadic hunters adapted to the extreme conditions. Today, most of them have settled for life in one place and have access to modern comforts. The groups include: the Inuits of the Canadian Far North and Greenland (150,000 people), the Sámi of Scandinavia and Russia (70,000 people), and, among the many Siberian peoples, the Dolgans (7,000 people). Only a third of the Sámi and some 250 Dolgans still live the nomadic life, shepherding reindeer.

The Animal Life (Fauna) of the Far North

Despite the harsh climate, many mammals live in the Arctic Circle, including some 25,000 polar bears, many of them in Canada. Canada is also home to wolves, arctic foxes, and small rodents called lemmings. The Siberian tundra is home to large herds of reindeer, many of them tame. In summer, migrant birds nest in the Far North. And the waters of the Arctic Ocean are rich in fish, particularly caplin and cod, which are hunted by colonies of seals and walrus.

The Plant Life (Flora) of the Far North

Neither deciduous trees nor conifers can survive in these latitudes. On the permanently frozen subsoil of the tundra, a mixture of mosses, lichens, and herbaceous plants turns green in summer and explodes into flower. These flowers are small and tough enough to survive the cold. There are also fungi and edible berries.

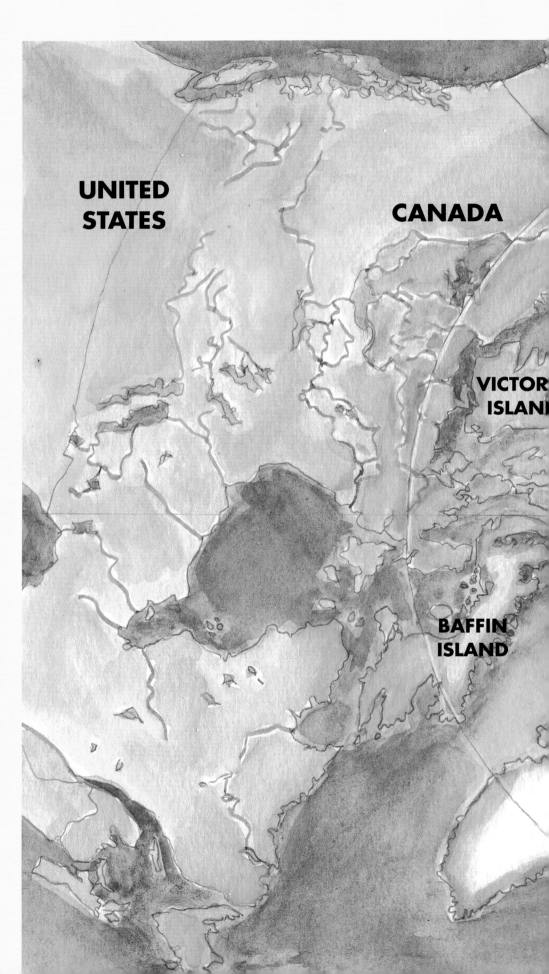

UNITED STATES

CANADA

VICTOR ISLAN

BAFFIN ISLAND

The glacial Arctic Ocean is the smallest ocean in the world at 5.7 million square miles. There is a deep basin in the center surrounded by the shallower waters of the continental shelf (land continuing below the ocean's surface). The circumpolar regions have an area of about 2.9 million square miles.

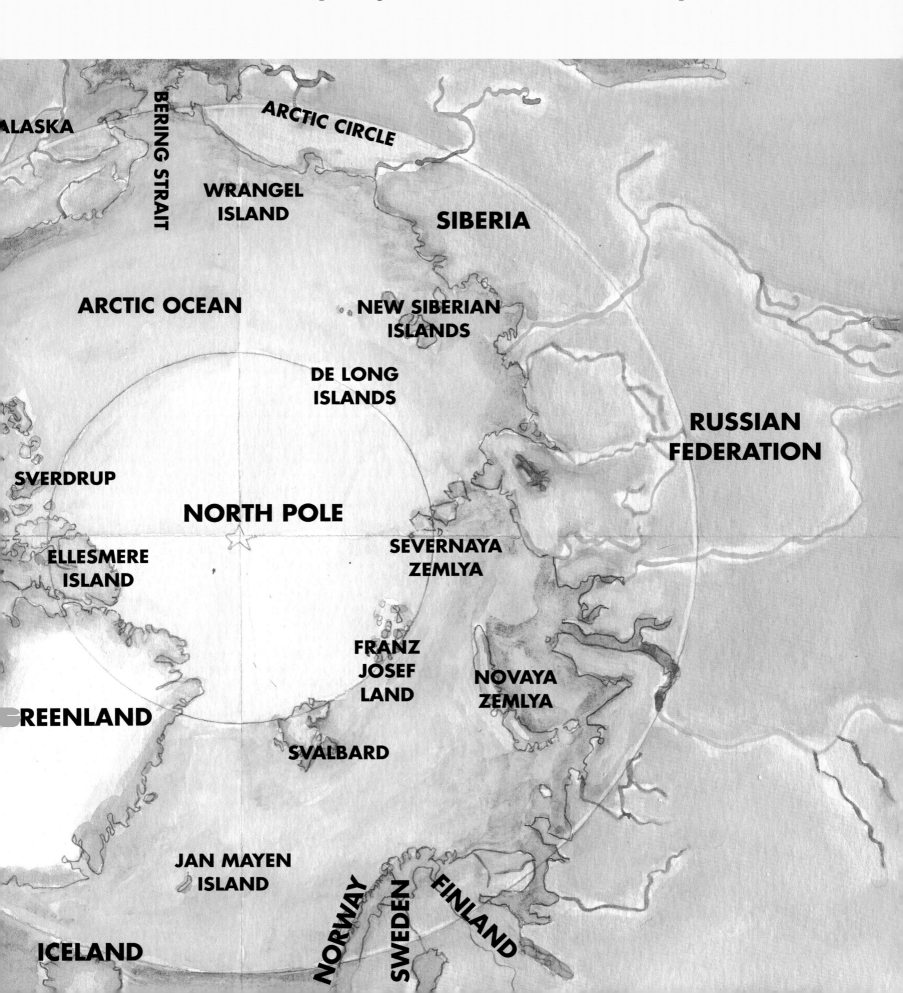

ALASKA

BERING STRAIT

ARCTIC CIRCLE

WRANGEL ISLAND

SIBERIA

ARCTIC OCEAN

NEW SIBERIAN ISLANDS

DE LONG ISLANDS

RUSSIAN FEDERATION

SVERDRUP

NORTH POLE

SEVERNAYA ZEMLYA

ELLESMERE ISLAND

FRANZ JOSEF LAND

NOVAYA ZEMLYA

REENLAND

SVALBARD

JAN MAYEN ISLAND

NORWAY

SWEDEN

FINLAND

ICELAND

The Regions of the Far North

The Arctic Ocean is partly frozen throughout the year. An ice sheet many feet deep forms on its surface. This sea of ice breaks up into enormous plates under the influence of the ocean currents.

The glacial Arctic Ocean is well named. Part of its surface, exposed to temperatures as low as –94° Fahrenheit, is permanently frozen. The North Pole, which lies on the latitude of 90° (90°N), is in the middle of this ice shelf; in other words, in the middle of the sea. It is a virtual geographical point used as a reference point in mapping the earth. There is nothing there to see.

Moving outward from the North Pole toward the Arctic Circle (the line within which the sun never rises in winter), we see land rising from the sea. These lands encircling the Arctic Ocean are called the circumpolar regions (regions around the Pole) and amount to some 2.9 million square miles. Most of this is composed of Alaska, the Canadian Far North, Scandinavian Lapland, and Siberia. To this we must add Greenland, the largest island in the world (840,000 square miles), and other smaller islands like the Queen Elizabeth Islands and the Novaya Zemlya and Spitzbergen archipelagos, or groups of islands.

These regions have certain things in common. Because they are so close to the Pole, their winter is one long polar night and their summer one long polar day. Vegetation is rare because of the cold. The only things that grow there are mosses, lichens, and some herbaceous plants.

The lands of the Arctic are a long way from the great capitals.

Sea Ice in Perpetual Motion

Sea ice is not frozen and immobile. Here you see it striated with cracks and channels.

Ice starts forming on the sea at 28° Fahrenheit. So a lot of ice forms on the Arctic Ocean! It forms a kind of shell over the sea, made from plates of ice that are constantly moved about by ocean currents and the wind. It is studded with chaotic blocks of ice that scientists call "pressure ridges." These occur when several sheets of ice collide and raft over each other or are forced upward. The ridges can be 30 feet high and several miles long. But the ice sheet can also be sufficiently smooth and sufficiently thick (10 to 15 feet) to form a landing strip for an aircraft. Sometimes it cracks and forms leads, or channels. Explorers need experience and caution in this unstable environment, where the landscape can change quite suddenly.

When the temperature rises in the summer, the ice sheet breaks up into floes and forms pack ice. The surface area of the sea ice varies with the seasons: In winter, it covers almost the entire Arctic Ocean. In summer, it covers only about 2 million square miles.

In summer, it is possible to use a kayak to move through the ice floes.

Breaking the Ice Sheet

Propelled by powerful motors, the icebreaker opens its own road through the thickest ice sheet, which it breaks beneath its own weight.

In the past, ships kept away from the Arctic Ocean in winter, when there was a danger of vessels being trapped and crushed by the ice floes. Many sailors lost their lives when their ships were wrecked in this way.

Icebreakers came into use at the beginning of the twentieth century to avert this danger. They are specially designed. The hull (the sloping sides of the ship) is reinforced with something like steel armor, the prow (front) of the ship is rounded to allow it to slide up over the ice and crush it, and the motors are very powerful so that the ship can move forward through the thickest ice.

One of the countries of the far north, Russia, has developed especially powerful icebreakers to allow ships to use its northern ports. The *Yamal* has nuclear motors with 75,000 horsepower, allowing it to take on ice floes several yards thick. These icebreakers transport food and equipment, and thanks to them, the Siberian coast is no longer so isolated during the long winter night. But the best way of getting around in the Arctic is by helicopter. Regular helicopter flights all around the frozen north are interrupted only by very bad weather. They bring the mail and supplies and can take the severely ill to the hospital.

There are no roads through the Russian tundra. Helicopters become "flying cabs."

The People of the Far North

The immense territories of the Arctic region are inhabited by several groups of people, including the Inuits, the Sámi, the Dolgans, and other Siberian peoples.

The Arctic peoples belong to a number of different countries and occupy different territories. They used to wander with their herds, a way of life called nomadic. But now they are mostly settled in one place. They live in villages and towns, though many often return to the ice sheet to renew their traditional way of life.

The Inuits (around 150,000 of them) live in Alaska, in Canada (particularly in Nunavut), and in Greenland (an autonomous province of Denmark). They used to be called Eskimos by their traditional foes, the Native Americans of Canada, and later by Westerners. But it is an insulting name that means "eaters of raw meat." Today they prefer to be called Inuit, which simply means "people." All young Inuits study English or Danish at school. But at home they speak Inuktitut, the Inuit language, whose alphabet has been modernized in order to make it computer-friendly.

The Sámi (formerly called Lapps) are native to Scandinavia. There are around 70,000 Sámi, and they live in the north of Norway, Sweden, Finland, and the Kola Peninsula in Russia. At school and at home, they speak one of the variants of Sámi, a Finno-Ungaric language.

Finally, of the twenty-six ethnic groups found in Siberia, there are some 7,000 Dolgans living in the Taimyr Peninsula (Russia), though only 250 of them are still nomads. They speak Russian and Yakut.

When Inuit children play cat's cradle, they represent animals like the fox or the caribou with its antlers.

A Long Migration Toward the East

These photos date from the 1930s, when the French explorer Paul-Émile Victor was studying the Eskimos of Greenland. At the time, almost nothing was known about their history and origins.

The ethnologist and explorer Paul-Émile Victor (1907–95) devoted part of his life to studying the Inuits of Greenland, who were at the time known as Eskimos. In 1934, he landed on the east shore of the island, at Ammasslik, where he spent the winter with the Inuits.

At that time, scientists were astonished by the presence of the Inuits, who have slanting eyes and Asiatic features, in Greenland. Today, it is thought that the first Inuits came from Mongolia, which lies between Russia and China. Traveling east, they probably crossed the Bering Strait from Russia to Alaska, where they first settled. Archaeological remains dating back to 10,000 BCE confirm their presence in Alaska. Scholars think that, hounded by the local Native Americans, the Inuits continued their migration across the Canadian Arctic to settle in Greenland between 2050 and 1700 BCE. Since then, they developed their ability to survive extremes of temperature and created what Victor called "the civilization of the seal": seals provide them with meat to eat, oil for lamps, and fur for clothing.

In the past, Inuit children traveled on their mothers' backs in the hoods of their garments.

Seals Populate the Ice Shelf

Seals like to lie out on the ice—in charmingly clumsy poses! But to find their food, these excellent swimmers must dive under the ice.

The seal belongs to the pinniped family and is a perfect example of a marine mammal. Seals are designed for swimming: their paddle-shaped tails drive them swiftly through the water, their ears are nothing more than holes that the water cannot penetrate, their eyes are adapted for underwater vision, and their nostrils can be closed by valves. As a result they can stay underwater for between forty-five minutes and two hours. During this time, they stuff themselves with fish, prawns, and crabs, before returning to the surface through a hole in the ice. On the surface, they run the danger of being spotted by hungry polar bears.

Six different species of seal live in the Arctic, each with its own rhythm of life. The harp seals (4.8 million animals) make an annual migration of 2,000 miles between the Arctic Ocean, their summer residence, and the Atlantic, where they spend the winter. In March and April, other common seal species, the bearded, ringed, and hooded seals, give birth to their young (called pups). The pups suckle for a few days to a month. The giant of the Arctic pinnipeds is the walrus, which boasts long ivory tusks. Unfortunately, as they were hunted by the Inuits for their meat and fat, they are on the brink of extinction. A few colonies of walrus survive in Greenland and Siberia.

The Inuit harpoon is terribly effective, even against the walrus, which can weigh up to a ton.

The Discovery of the Arctic

Venturing into the Arctic, sailors and explorers braved great danger. Even today, a boat is sometimes trapped by the shifting ice.

Explorers discovered the northern regions of the globe very early in human history. The earliest known explorer was a Greek, Pytheas the Massaliot, who left Marseilles aboard his oared galley. In 330 BCE, he reached the "land of Thule," supposedly the Faroe Islands. Much later, in 982 CE, the Viking Erik the Red "discovered" Greenland.

From the sixteenth century on, navigators tried to locate or open a passage through the ice. Some sought the Northeastern Passage along the Siberian coast; others sought the Northwestern Passage along the North American coast. Such a passage would make it easier to trade with people on the other side of the world. And many died in the attempt, among them the Dutchman Willem Barents, who discovered Spitzbergen in 1597; the Englishman Henry Hudson, who came within 660 miles of the North Pole in 1607; and the Dane Vitus Bering, who died in 1741 having crossed the strait between the American and Asian continents and given his name to it—the Bering Strait.

Only in 1893–96 did the Norwegian Fridtjof Nansen discover the existence of the glacial Arctic Ocean. For three years, he let his ship, the *Fram*, drift along with the ocean currents. When it was trapped by the pack ice, he spent the winter on the ice in temperatures of –40° Fahrenheit. On his return to Norway, he was greeted as a hero.

Even today, pack ice is a danger to ships and can trap the unsuspecting.

The Conquest of the North Pole

The Pole is simply a geographical point on the ice sheet at 90° North. But the difficulty of attaining it made it an obsession with nineteenth-century explorers.

In the early twentieth century, it was every explorer's dream to reach the mythical North Pole. One such man, Robert Edwin Peary, was determined that he would be the first to do so. He tried to reach it seven times! Then he resolved that the year 1909 would make his name famous forever . . .

On March 1, 1909, Peary had reached the latitude of 87° 47' North. He was only 125 miles from the Pole. He prepared his sleighs for the final approach across the ice. Four Inuits and his faithful servant, Matthew Henson, went with him. On April 6, 1909, at ten in the morning, he achieved his greatest dream: he reached the North Pole. But when he returned to civilization, a terrible disappointment awaited him. The newspapers, which he had not read during his expedition, were full of the exploits of another American explorer, Frederick Cook, who claimed to have reached the Pole on April 21 of the previous year. A fierce argument broke out between the two men. Eventually, the experts decided in Peary's favor and he was declared the first man to reach the North Pole. But specialists today think that he did not have time, between March and April 1909, to reach the Pole and return. That would have meant an exhausting 250 mile return trip over the ice.

Since this unfortunate quarrel, a number of men have reached the North Pole. In 1986, the Frenchman Jean-Louis Étienne reached it solo on skis.

The compass points to the magnetic North Pole, which is hundreds of miles from the geographic Pole.

Bitter Cold

The very low temperatures make the Arctic climate almost unendurable. Blizzards, wind, snow, and fog are common. Survival is possible only by protecting oneself from the cold.

The lack of sunlight explains the harsh climate of the Arctic. The sun never rises high enough in the sky to warm the atmosphere. There are two main seasons: winter and summer. In winter, the days are short and the nights very long. The average temperature is –13° Fahrenheit. Winter lasts about six months. During the three months of summer, the nights are very short, the days very long and bright, and the temperatures rarely go higher than 50°. Between the two, spring and autumn last only a few short weeks each.

The Arctic climate is very dry. Sea water (because it is salt water) freezes at 28° and, once frozen, does not evaporate. Without humidity, there are few clouds in the sky and precipitation (water falling as rain or snow) is rare. Less than 10 inches of water a year falls in the Far North. In this, it paradoxically resembles the arid expanses of the Sahara desert!

These climatic conditions have allowed the formation of glaciers. Successive layers of snow, building up to hundreds of yards in depth, have, over several million years, produced these rivers of ice.

This Dolgan is battling the cold. His eyes are protected from the very intense sunlight by dark glasses.

The Work of the Wind

The winds of the Arctic region are very strong. They sculpt the ice into strange and magnificent forms. But they are also very dangerous!

It is one of the mysteries of the Arctic: a wind can suddenly rise, instantly conjuring severe weather conditions from a clear, blue sky.

Of all the Arctic winds, the blizzard is the best known. It brings with it squalls of snow that limit visibility and hide every landmark. Sometimes you can barely see your own feet!

Catabatic winds can occur in the Arctic. Air cooled by a glacier flows down the slope of the ice sheet toward the shore, gaining speed as it goes. They can attain very high speeds and have been known to carry away whole buildings!

The most violent winds in the northern hemisphere are found in Greenland, especially in the Amassalik region on the east side of the island: peak speeds of 190 miles per hour have been recorded.

The strength of the wind intensifies one's sense of cold. This is called the windchill factor, and scientists have made a table of its effects. The "bite" of the wind is measured in terms of air temperature and the speed of the wind. Thus a blizzard blowing at 40 miles per hour with an air temperature of 68° Fahrenheit will produce a sensation of cold on the skin equivalent to a temperature of −56°.

And it is by "biting" the ice that the wind sculpts these strange forms and fantastical animals.

The gusting wind raises swirls of snow and creates "white light."

Dressing Warmly

These Dolgans look very handsome in their everyday wear made of reindeer hide, with matching boots and mittens.

Wearing furs is still the best way of protecting yourself from the extreme cold of the Arctic. Animal hides are warm, durable, and waterproof. Like the other natives of the Arctic, the Dolgans learned early on to tan, cut, and sew garments of leather. Among the Dolgans, these tasks are carried out by women.

Every group has its own traditions. The Inuits tend to wear jackets and anoraks of sealskin, a very supple leather from which they also make mittens and boots. The Dolgans, like the Sámi, use the skin of the reindeer, which wander over the tundra in herds. But all these groups take great care with their appearance and love embroidery, wooden and metal charms, and beads. In the past, they acquired them by bartering for them with furs with the few foreign traders who came this far north. These days the Dolgans buy them in Khatanga, the capital of the Russian province of Taimyr. But what they most prize is white fur, since the color white is supposed to deter evil spirits; the best thing of all is the fluffy tail of the Arctic fox.

An Inuit family may dress in nothing but furs. The men wear trousers made of polar-bear skin.

His Majesty the Polar Bear

The polar bear is the lord and master of his ice-shelf hunting grounds. Majestic, often solitary, he rules here by virtue of his strength. He has no enemy or predator but humankind.

The polar bear is not exactly cuddly! The biggest carnivore (meat eater) on land, the male polar bear can weigh up to 1,300 pounds and the female up to 880. When the male stands upright, he is more than six feet tall and can look an elephant in the eye.

The polar bear is a living symbol of the Arctic. Its Latin name is *Ursus maritimus*. This is a creature perfectly adapted to the climate: Its coat is very warm, and a thick layer of fat beneath affords further insulation from the cold. Its big, webbed feet make the polar bear an excellent swimmer.

Most of its time is spent hunting seals on the ice shelf. Its fine sense of smell allows it to detect a seal up to 18 miles away. A single blow of the bear's massive claws dispatches the seal, which is then eaten.

When the ice shelf melts in the summer, polar bears take refuge on the coast. There is little for them to eat then, and they survive on berries, seaweed, and fish. This is when the female digs out a den for herself and gives birth to her cubs. A newborn cub is hardly bigger than a kitten.

There are still about 25,000 polar bears in the Arctic. They live mainly in Greenland, on the shore of Hudson Bay (Canada), and on the Norwegian island of Spitzbergen.

This "tundra buggy" from Churchill, a town in the Canadian Far North, allows people to get quite close to bears.

Hunting with the Inuits

For the Inuits of today, the hunt has lost none of its thrills. They sledge for dozens of miles over the ice in the hope of killing a seal or a bear.

The Inuits have always been great hunters. Their way of life has changed, but they still have the right to kill bears and seals in their own territories. In early March, when the days start to lengthen, the men prepare their sled harnesses. The sled dogs are huskies, dogs once crossbred with wolves, and true athletes. Six dogs pull a sled; they can cover 60 miles and go without food for two or three days. They drink by lapping up the snow while still on the run. The lead dog, chosen for its strength and intelligence, is an important guide. He picks his way carefully over the ice floes.

At this time of year, the ice shelf is still solid. It will melt only in May, when summer comes. Until then, the Inuit hunting grounds expand greatly!

Seals are hunted for their flesh, oil, and fur. They come up for air and sun themselves on the ice, but they are wary and must be approached very carefully. The Inuit hunters advance behind a little white veil that makes them, from the seal's point of view, invisible.

Sometimes the Inuits come across the fresh tracks of a polar bear. Tracking it down is dangerous but exciting. If they make a kill, the bear meat will be shared among all the inhabitants of the village.

The sled dogs are trained to be tough. They sleep outside even in winter and are fed dried fish.

The *Inlandis* of Greenland

In the Arctic, the land is covered with snow or ice throughout most of the year. Firns, or névés (beds of porous ice, not yet compacted into glacier ice), combine with the glaciers to create landscapes of dazzling beauty.

Early in the Quaternary Era, about 4.1 million years ago, the climate was much colder than it is today. Monstrous glaciers that we call *inlandis* covered a large part of Europe and America. Most of these have now disappeared, the exceptions being in Greenland in the north and in Antarctica in the south.

Greenland's *inlandis* has been formed over more than two million years. An enormously thick layer of ice covers most of the island: the icecap. This dome-shaped mass covers 650,000 square miles; at its thickest, it is over two miles deep.

Under its weight, the center of Greenland has been flattened like a biscuit and pushed 1,000 feet below sea level.

This *inlandis* is about 650,000 cubic miles in volume and represents some 9 percent of the earth's reserve of fresh water.

Dragged downward by their weight, the glaciers of the ice cap move very slowly. As they move, they wear down (erode) the mountains that they cover. A very few rocky peaks, called nunataks, stick out through the ice.

Closer to the coast, glaciers reach fjords (former glacial valleys invaded by the sea). There they break up and melt in the sea. This is the source of the gigantic icebergs that drift out into the ocean under the influence of winds and currents.

The Inuits mark out paths with stone landmarks, which they call *inuksuk*, meaning "manlike."

Cathedrals of Ice

These impressive cliffs of ice are true floating islands. The icebergs from the Arctic travel long distances on the open sea before melting away.

Unlike the ice shelf, which is formed of frozen seawater, icebergs are made of fresh water. This is because the glaciers from which they're formed are made of snow, not frozen seawater. Icebergs float because ice is lighter than water. The biggest of them rise some 230 feet from the surface of the sea. But only a part of the iceberg is visible; the underwater part represents some seven eighths of these great objects. The colors of these cathedrals of ice vary with the light, covering the whole spectrum of blue from a translucent blue-green to an almost metallic gray-blue.

Some 90 percent of the big icebergs adrift in the North Atlantic come from the east coast of Greenland, notably from the wonderfully beautiful glacier of Sermeq Kujalleq. The other 10 percent come from the Arctic islands east of Canada.

Icebergs travel at an average speed of 0.4 miles per hour. Their speed depends on the strength of the winds and currents driving them. They sometimes reach New York in the United States, there to melt away 2,500 miles from their source. In 1912, the ocean liner *Titanic* sank after hitting an iceberg near Newfoundland. Today, ships are warned of approaching icebergs by their radar.

In the past, these mountains of ice would suddenly loom out of the fog, leaving the helmsman no time to avoid them.

In the Wake of the Whale

This humpback whale has surfaced off the coast of Greenland in order to breathe. It blasts a jet of water into the air, before diving back down to the depths with a great sweep of its tail.

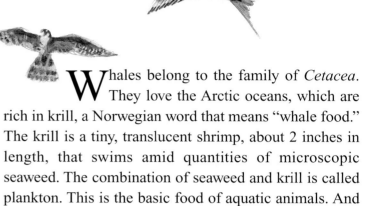

Whales belong to the family of *Cetacea*. They love the Arctic oceans, which are rich in krill, a Norwegian word that means "whale food." The krill is a tiny, translucent shrimp, about 2 inches in length, that swims amid quantities of microscopic seaweed. The combination of seaweed and krill is called plankton. This is the basic food of aquatic animals. And whales do not hold back on their krill intake!

Whales are among the largest living creatures on the planet. They can be up to 100 feet long and weigh up to 150 tons.

Whales were long hunted for their very fatty flesh, from which oil was extracted. Whales also have a kind of very stiff barrier of hair that filters what comes into their mouth, and these "baleens" were used to make the struts of umbrellas and to stiffen women's corsets. In the nineteenth century, whale hunting became an industry and flotillas of whaling ships scoured the seas. Between 1925 and 1975, more than 1.5 million whales were killed. Consequently, about thirty species of whale are now on the verge of extinction.

In 1986, an international agreement ended the massacre for a while. Unfortunately, some countries, notably Japan, do not respect the agreement and continue to hunt whales.

Every year, 9 million tourists travel to see whales.

Color in the Night

Every year, the natives of the Arctic experience the long, dark polar night. So they bring as much color as they can into their daily lives, painting their houses in vivid shades.

The Arctic people used to be nomads. Whole families would move around the ice shelf, following the hunting and fishing. Today, they are almost all sedentary, living in towns and enjoying the comforts of urban life.

In Greenland, the Inuits live in coastal villages where they have access to supplies brought by sea. Their well-heated houses have telephone and Internet access. Sometimes, the villagers still get together to eat raw seal meat after a successful hunt.

Even town-dwelling Inuits tend to spend their holidays hunting. In winter, hunters build a place where they can rest and take shelter from the storms: an igloo. They cut out blocks of compacted snow with a saw and pile them up into a dome shape.

In 1999, the Canadian Inuits obtained (after long years of negotiation with the government) their own self-ruled territory, the Nunavut, meaning "our land." It covers 733,000 square miles of northwest Canada. About one fifth of the population (4,500 out of the 26,600 Canadian Inuits) lives in the capital, Iqaluit.

An igloo takes about three hours to build. Well insulated, it helps conserve body heat and affords protection from the cold.

The Dolgans: Nomads of the Tundra

In the Taimyr Peninsula (Russia), reindeer are harnessed as horses used to be in Europe. These tame ruminants (animals that chew cud) pull the tents of nomadic Dolgans across the tundra.

The Dolgans are among the last nomadic herders to shepherd their reindeer year-round over the plains of Taimyr in Siberia. In winter, the reindeer can still find mosses and lichens to eat beneath the snow, but every fortnight they and their shepherds must move on in search of new pastures. At each migration, they travel some 5 to 10 miles across the frozen tundra before setting up a new camp.

Their tents—which are more like little houses—are called *baloks*; each is pulled along by a team of eight reindeer. Mounted on runners, they slide over the snow like a sled. Entire families (as many as five to seven people each) live in these tiny dwellings, which are made of a wood frame covered with reindeer hide and heated by a wood-burning stove with a metal chimney. The Dolgans also cook at this stove. In summer, they use a lighter tent.

This way of life has continued for over two hundred years. But only about 250 Dolgans maintain this lifestyle, called transhumance. The others prefer the easier life of the city.

The few Dolgans who continue with the nomadic lifestyle live for their reindeer and take very good care of their herds.

The Reindeer of the Tundra

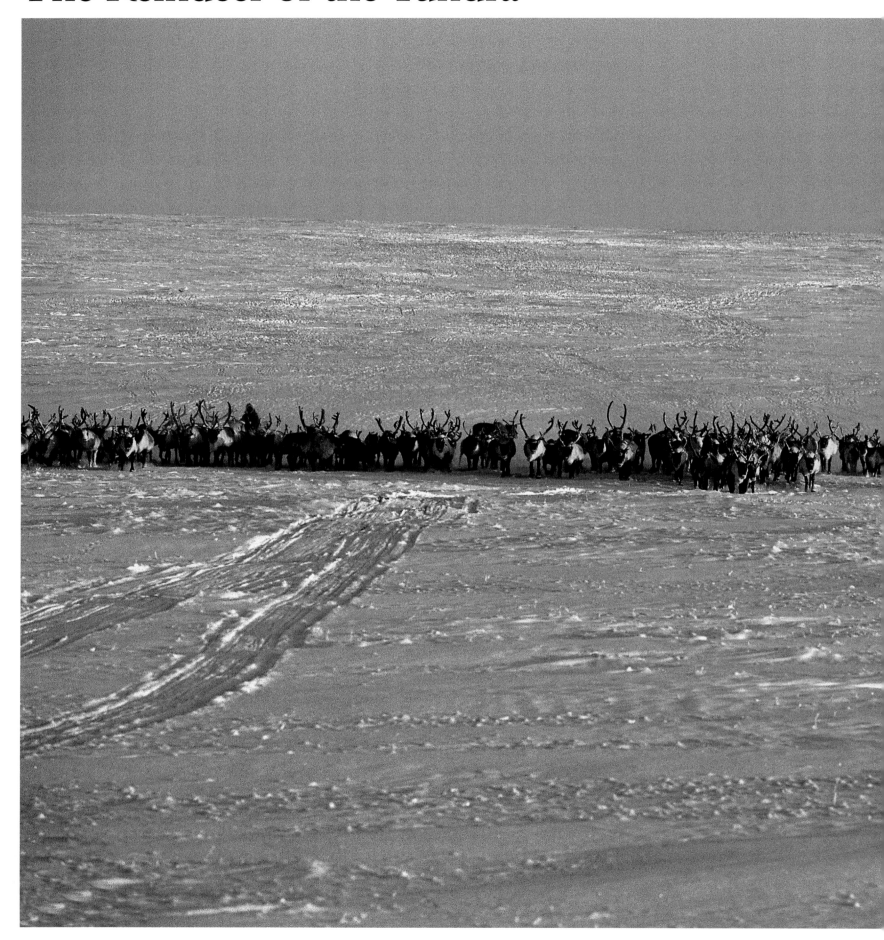

The vast herds of reindeer seek food under the snow of the Siberian tundra. But food is scarce, which means that the herds must regularly move on when the food is exhausted.

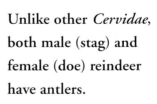

Reindeer, found in northern Europe and Asia, and caribou, found in northern America, are not identical but are almost the same species. They belong to the family *Cervidae* and, their heads crowned with majestic antlers, are tundra royalty. The horns, or antlers, they grow are made of bone irrigated by blood vessels. They change color with the seasons, from red to dark brown, fall off during the winter, and regrow over the following year. This cumbersome body part is a weapon. Male reindeer use it to fight and impose their rule on the herd. In the mating season, the herd champion acquires his own group of females.

In winter, wild reindeer, which can weigh up to 450 pounds, find their food under the snow. They scratch with their hooves to expose the buried mosses and lichens. When the snow is frozen solid, they can no longer do this, and so they set off on long migrations across the vast frozen plains of Siberia in search of softer snow.

The Sámi and the Siberian tribes have long had domesticated reindeer. They milk them and live on their meat.

Unlike other *Cervidae*, both male (stag) and female (doe) reindeer have antlers.

A Day in the Life of the Dolgans

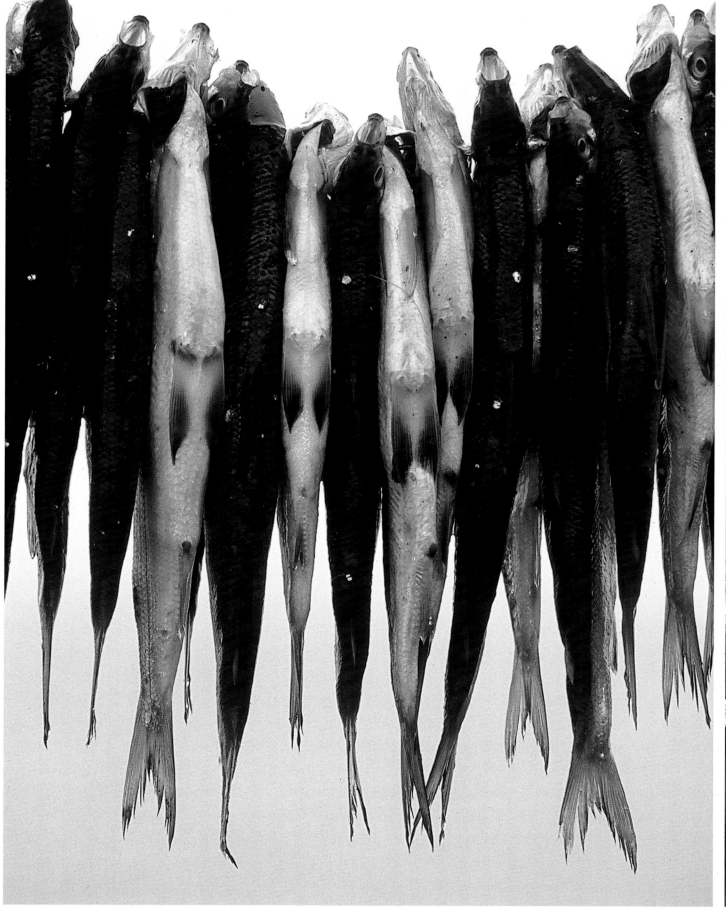

Fish dry in the winds of the tundra. The Dolgans' nomadic lifestyle means that they must provide for almost all their own needs.

Dolgan cattle breeders live completely independent of other people in the tundra. What they need, they must find or make for themselves. Every day, as they shepherd their reindeer herds, they set traps to catch fur-bearing animals. They generally catch foxes or wolves but sometimes land a bear. Carrying it back to the camp, they cut up the dead animal and eat what they can of it, then tan the hide. The resulting furs are valuable; in the past, they were bartered for other goods, but now they are sold in towns. Tradition required that a Dolgan man offer a bear skin to the woman he wanted to marry.

In summer, the Dolgans fish in lakes and rivers. Their catches, gutted and dried in the open air, are eaten by the entire community. In the Taimyr Peninsula, a traditional recipe called stroganina is made of fish of the *Salmondidae* family: the trout, char, and salmon of freshwater streams. The fish is stripped of its scales and frozen. Then it is cut up, still frozen, into fine flakes and served with pepper and salt. Tea or vodka is served with stroganina. It takes a little getting used to!

In Canada, the Inuits of Nunavut sculpt and sell objects in a stone called steatite, or soapstone.

The Polar Night

In winter, the sun doesn't rise on the Arctic. It is night almost all the time. But above the Siberian tundra, the Northern Lights cover the sky in narrow bands of color.

The polar night and its opposite, the "midnight sun," are explained by the rotation of the earth around the sun. The axis about which the earth rotates is at an angle to that of the sun. This is what gives the seasons their rhythm: the shortening of daylight in the winter and the longer days of summer. At the equator, days last twelve hours all year round and do not vary with the season. At the poles, the shortening and lengthening of daylight is at its most extreme.

In the northern hemisphere, between September 23 and March 31, the sun does not rise on regions north of the Arctic Circle (66.33°N). There are 174 days of almost total darkness at the North Pole and 90 days at Thule (Qaanaaq), in Greenland, the world's most northerly town (76°N). Daylight very gradually returns.

One of the most spectacular features of the polar night is the Northern Lights, or aurora borealis. Long fluorescent veils—green, yellow, or blue—undulate in the sky for minutes at a time. These curtains of light were once considered magical. Now we know that they form in the ionosphere, one of the upper layers of the atmosphere, at an altitude of 50 to 100 miles. Electrons, accelerated by the combined magnetic spheres of the sun and earth, collide with atoms of gas; these atoms give off light like the gas in a fluorescent tube.

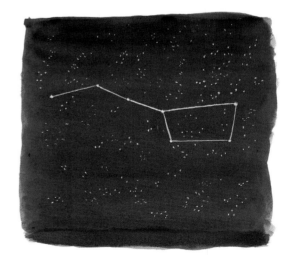

The Great Bear is particularly clear in the Arctic sky. The ancient Greeks called it arctos, or bear, which is the origin of the word *arctic*.

Siberian Festival

Today is a festival in this little Siberian village. They are celebrating the return of the sun after the long polar night. The Dolgans gather to sing and dance before sitting down to a feast.

In late February or early March, the Arctic world celebrates the return of the sun, which begins its slow reconquest of the sky. The days lengthen, and the light returns. The date of these festivities varies from country to country, but they happen everywhere in the Arctic.

In the Taimyr Peninsula, where the Dolgans live, the return of the sun is marked by open-air dancing. Then a great straw man is burned to symbolize the "death" of winter. Lasso competitions are organized. The idea is to throw the noose around the legs of a galloping animal and stop it in its tracks. Dolgan men are amazingly good at this.

The festivities extend into the evening. For both the Inuits and the Dolgans, the most important traditional instruments are the trumpet and the drum. The drum is shallow and made of taut reindeer hide; it looks like a tambourine and sometimes has little bells attached to it. It beats out the rhythm and supports the choral song. But it is also an instrument of communication with the spirits. Shamans (witch doctors) sometimes enter a special mental state, called a trance, when playing it.

For the festival, the Greenland women wear their traditional red and white costumes.

The Arctic Summer

The sun slowly returns. The snow melts, flows away, and evaporates. In June, the Arctic summer makes its appearance. All of a sudden, the tundra is covered with a short-lived tapestry of flowers.

It is as if the arrival of summer produces an explosion of joy in the Arctic regions. Nature itself seems to rejoice! The tundra is defined by its permafrost, which means that the soil under the surface is permanently frozen. But the surface melts in summer, creating shallow marshland. The frozen ground melts and suddenly returns to life. It shelters a million sleeping seeds that seek new life. In a matter of a few weeks, there is astounding growth, fueled by the almost continuous sunlight of the midnight sun. Many plants flower: the yellow and the white poppy, the red willow, the mauve willow-herb. Some of these are useful: the shaggy head of cotton grass served in the past to line Inuit boots. Bilberry and other berries abound, as do fungi such as the edible boletus.

Animals, too, take advantage of the summery conditions. Migrating birds, which spend the winter in the warm south, return to the Arctic. Terns and auks make their nests. The rich insect life of summer provides food for the nestlings. There are swarms of mosquitoes everywhere. They even bother the reindeer and can drive them mad!

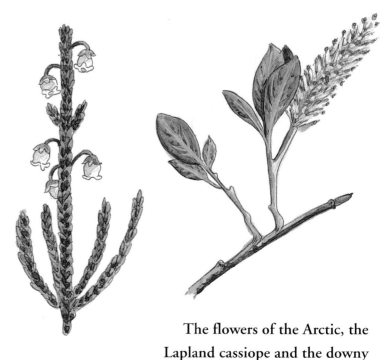

The flowers of the Arctic, the Lapland cassiope and the downy willow, are small and sturdy.

A Herd of Musk Oxen

The wild, shaggy musk oxen wander in serried ranks through the Arctic tundra. Here they are seen in the Taimyr Peninsula.

Squat and short-legged, buried in its mass of hair, the musk ox is designed for the Far North, where it lives in herds. It is a ruminant, like the reindeer, and loves to graze the tundra. It scratches the snow with its broad hooves to uncover the lichens and mosses that it feeds on. Males can weigh up to 750 pounds and have a profound sense of community. To defend themselves again wolves, their main predators, they form a circle, in the center of which they place females and young. Then they confront the enemy with their long, sharp horns. Males also fight one another for females during the mating season in late summer. They then give off a very powerful scent called "musk," which gives them their name and is intended to attract the female musk ox.

The fleece of the musk ox is like a wonderfully thick, dense sweater that keeps body heat in. But it is not very good against rain; the soaked hairs freeze when the cold returns and the animal can die of hypothermia (extreme cold).

The virtues of musk-ox fur (the warmest in the world, with individual hairs up to 90 centimeters long) attracted trappers, and the animal was hunted to the brink of extinction. It is now protected. It lives free in Alaska and Canada, in particular on Banks Island, which has 68,000 of them. It was reintroduced into Siberia in 1970.

Musk oxen renew their coat every year in the molting season.

Pacifying the Evil Spirits

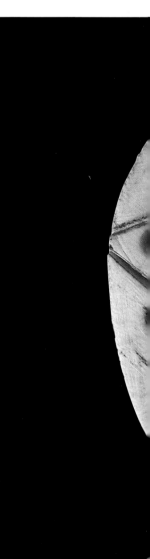

Arctic peoples believe that jewels and amulets will protect them against evil spirits. Amazing fact: the Dolgans of Siberia sculpt these objects in mammoth ivory!

Throughout the Arctic region, the shaman is greatly respected. He is the religious chief of a clan or village. The Dolgans, like the Inuits and the Sámi, are animists who believe that nature is inhabited by spirits. They are particularly wary of the hidden spirits that haunt the tundra and the glaciers, believing that only the shaman can communicate with these all-powerful beings. Cajoling the spirits with offerings, the shaman cures illnesses by magic and wards off the spells that threaten the shep-herd and his reindeer herd.

To avert these evil spells, animists perform many different kinds of rituals. For example, the Dolgans always walk around a sacred site in a particular direction (clockwise or counterclockwise). They avoid coming close to a rock under which an evil spirit might be sleeping. They also invoke the spirit of fire, asking him to keep their possessions safe—first and foremost, their little house on runners, the *balok*.

The Dolgans also wear amulets. In the Taimyr Peninsula of Siberia, these little objects, a kind of good-luck charm, are sculpted in mammoth ivory, the only valuable material found in the region. Mammoths were a kind of prehistoric elephant. When they died, their bodies were preserved by the cold and remained buried in the tundra as if in a freezer. From time to time, the Dolgans unearth a mammoth bone or tusk and put it to use.

The Dolgans organize shamanic ceremonies to drive out evil spirits.

A Mammoth Called Jarkov

A very old mammoth is concealed inside this block of ice. His impressive tusks are sticking out. He died some 20,000 years ago, and his body has been preserved intact by the extreme cold of Siberia.

The story of this extraordinary scientific discovery begins in December 1997. Bernard Buigues, a French expert on fossils (paleontologist), was working in the Taimyr Peninsula. One morning, he tripped over a big piece of bone in the frozen tundra. At first, he had no thought that it might be a mammoth. But the Dolgans, who know that such frozen beasts occasionally turn up in this region, were quick to show him another site nearby, where a pair of tusks some ten feet long was sticking up!

Money had to be found for the Mammuthus expedition, and in September 1999, a team of scientists set up a base in Khatanga, the main town of the region. With the temperature at –40°, it took five weeks with pneumatic drills to cut open the earth around the frozen mammoth. Finally, on October 17, 1999, the mastodon, still in its enormous block of ice, was winched up by a very powerful helicopter. It was transported to Khatanga, where a special underground laboratory with a constant temperature of –15° was built to hold it. Scientists can now study it without it decomposing (rotting away).

It has been dubbed Jarkov after the last name of the Dolgan who found it. Having examined it, the scientists concluded that Jarkov died at the age of forty-seven a mere 20,380 years ago.

Jarkov was surrounded by a twenty-ton block of ice. He himself weighs three tons!

Scientific Expeditions

A few tents standing in the vast white plains of the Taimyr Peninsula are the only outward sign of a major scientific campaign to understand the mysteries of the Arctic.

The Arctic glaciers and the frozen subsoil of the tundra afford new possibilities for contemporary science. The glaciers were formed tens of millions of years ago, and the cold has conserved rare traces of that remote past. They are therefore like a time machine, allowing us access to prehistory. Core samples taken by drilling down into the depths of the *inlandis* in Greenland offer cylindrical cross-sections of this past and help scientists understand aspects of prehistory such as climate.

Many countries take part in this research, and this international cooperation is not new. It began with the International Polar Year (IPY), a program of research into the polar regions, in 1882–83. There was a second IPY in 1932–33 and a third in 1957–58. The next is scheduled for 2007–08. Presided over by the United Nations Educational, Scientific and Cultural Organization (UNESCO), it will bring together scientists from more than thirty countries. Their goal is to understand the role of the polar climate in regulating the climate of the rest of the world and to evaluate the threat of global warming.

Warmly wrapped up though they are, the scientists cannot avoid ice forming on their mustaches.

Heat Wave in the Arctic

These metalworks in Norilsk in northern Russia represent industry's contribution to global warming. Their toxic fumes are serious pollutants, and the Arctic is suffering.

After much calculation, scientists have come to the conclusion that earth's climate is warming and that much of this warming is due to the carbon dioxide (CO_2) emitted by cars, planes, and factories. What is more, these effects are twice as clear at the two poles as they are anywhere else on the planet. Figures published in 2004 by the Arctic Climate Impact Assessment (ACIA), an American research institute, show that temperatures have increased by an average of 4° Fahrenheit in Alaska and Siberia over the last fifty years. Over the same period, the Arctic ice shelf has diminished by more than 6 percent in area and 40 percent in depth.

Greenland's *inlandis* has also begun to melt. Elsewhere, the frozen subsoil is beginning to melt. The thawing of the subsoil might produce a catastrophe by releasing methane gas until now held captive by the permafrost. Methane, or marsh gas, which is produced underground by the rotting of plant matter, is itself an agent in the process of global warming. It could establish a vicious cycle: methane release would accelerate global warming, releasing more and more methane. The celebrated astrophysicist Hubert Reeves calls this process "a sleeping dragon" that we should take care not to wake.

Not all pollution is airborne. An oil tanker pollutes everything around it when it runs aground.

The Threat to Animal Life

This handsome bear sculpted in ice is doomed to disappear. Global warming will melt it. And if the ice shelf can no longer form because of increasing temperatures, the polar bear, too, will disappear.

The animals of the Arctic are unprepared for global warming, which destroys their ways of life. Polar bears are among the first victims. If the ice shelf contracts, so does their food supply. By devouring the seals that they find on the ice between November and May, they build up stocks of fat that allow them to survive the summer months, when they can find little to eat.

With their winter feeding season at risk, polar bears are living on borrowed time. According to the Canadian Wildlife Service, the 12,000 bears recorded west of Hudson Bay are already showing signs of weakness. Undernourished females are too weak to have offspring or to feed their cubs properly if any are born. Bear birthrates are falling, and the scrawny cubs are 15 percent below their expected weight. If nothing is done, extinction is inevitable.

The reindeer of the tundra are not much better off. The herds suffer from an indirect consequence of global warming: ice. The subsoil thaws at 32° Fahrenheit but quickly freezes over again when the temperature falls. But the ice formed after the thaw is much harder than snow, and the reindeer are not strong enough to break it with their hooves in order to reach their food. The reindeer are dying, and the size of herds is gradually falling.

Famished polar bears sometimes scavenge from trash cans in the hope of finding food.

The Polar World Adrift

Will these ice floes adrift on the Arctic Ocean disappear as a result of global warming? That would mean the end of the polar region as we know it—and would have alarming consequences for the rest of the world.

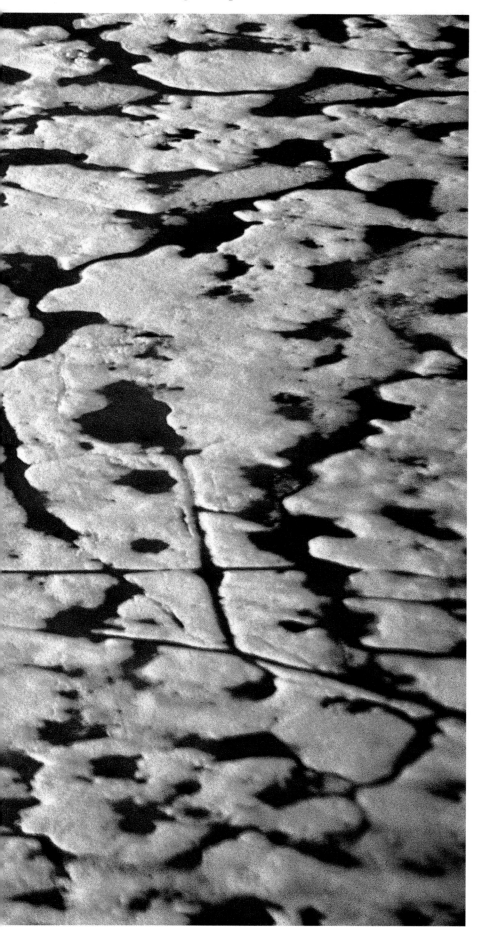

If the ice shelf of the North Pole and the *inlandis* of Greenland were both to melt, the sea level would rise by 20 feet throughout the world. Entire countries that now lie just above sea-level, such as Bangladesh and the Maldive Islands in Asia, would be overrun by the ocean.

Fortunately, this is still a distant prospect. But ecologists and scientists are very worried about the thaw that has begun in the Arctic ice sheets. The freshwater liberated by this thaw flows into the oceans and modifies their salinity (the amount of salt in seawater). This change is already disturbing the life cycles of certain fishes such as cod, which are becoming rarer.

The change would also affect the Gulf Stream, the warm ocean current to which Western Europe owes its temperate climate. The Gulf Stream flows where it does because of a combination of water temperature and salinity. If the balance were altered, it might have important consequences, altering the flow of the stream. For the time being, no one can say what these would be. But they might mean that Great Britain and the Atlantic Coast of Europe would undergo further climate changes, with very hot summers and very cold winters.

Greenlanders like to melt and drink the very pure water of the *inlandis*.

The Future of the Great North

What is this Dolgan child dreaming of as he shepherds the reindeer? Perhaps he is thinking of growing up in the tundra and becoming a nomadic herder like his parents. But will he be able to?

The native peoples of the Arctic are very attached to their traditions and ways of life. For a long time, they lived isolated from the rest of the world by physical distance. But now, with the advent of the telephone and Internet, the Arctic peoples have established communications; they know about each other and are organizing to publicize their cultures—and save them.

Though they are of various nationalities (American, Canadian, Danish, Finnish, Norwegian, Russian, and Swedish), they have begun a joint effort to save their region from the threat of global warming. But they have not found it easy to make themselves heard; they are few, and are therefore considered tiny minorities on the global stage.

However, their representatives have tried to plead their cause in major international forums, such as the United Nations (UN). Theirs is the environment that will be most immediately affected. But they point out that, if things continue as they are, everyone else will be affected, too . . .

The peoples of the Arctic form one large family, and they are determined to pool their forces and defend their future.